Sir Talkalot
and
the Dragon

A humorous
fantasy story

First published in 2005 by
Franklin Watts
338 Euston Road
London
NW1 3BH

Franklin Watts Australia
Level 17 / 207 Kent Street
Sydney
NSW 2000

A CIP catalogue record for this book is available
from the British Library.

ISBN 978 0 7496 6130 4

Series Editor: Jackie Hamley
Series Advisors: Dr Barrie Wade, Dr Hilary Minns
Design: Peter Scoulding

Printed in China

Franklin Watts is a division of
Hachette Children's Books,
an Hachette UK company.
www.hachette.co.uk

Sir Talkalot
and the Dragon

Written by
Sherryl Clark

Illustrated by
Neil Chapman

W
FRANKLIN WATTS
LONDON•SYDNEY

Sherryl Clark

"I like to read in bed. Sometimes it sends me to sleep, but sometimes an exciting book will keep me awake. I can't bear to stop reading!"

Neil Chapman

"I love to draw dragons. Like people, they come in so many shapes, sizes and colours. And if you know a dragon, you will always be invited to barbecues!"

Sir Talkalot was a brave knight
but he talked – a lot.

Every day he put people to sleep
with his long, boring stories.

One day, news came of a dragon
causing trouble in a far-off village.

The King sent Sir Talkalot to help.

When Sir Talkalot arrived,
he saw a terrible sight.

"What happened?" he asked.

"Did the dragon attack you?"

"No," said the mayor.

"The dragon can't get to sleep.
But he's so tired, he keeps
falling over," explained
the mayor.

15

Sir Talkalot didn't want to kill the dragon just for being tired.

But something had to be done.

"I'll try talking to him," he said.

So Sir Talkalot climbed all the
way up to the dragon's cave.

The dragon looked very grumpy.
"Go away!" he growled.

Sir Talkalot drew his sword.

Then he had another idea.

"Let me tell you about the time I won the Knight of the Year Award," he said.

"Oh no!" groaned the dragon.

But Sir Talkalot began his tale.

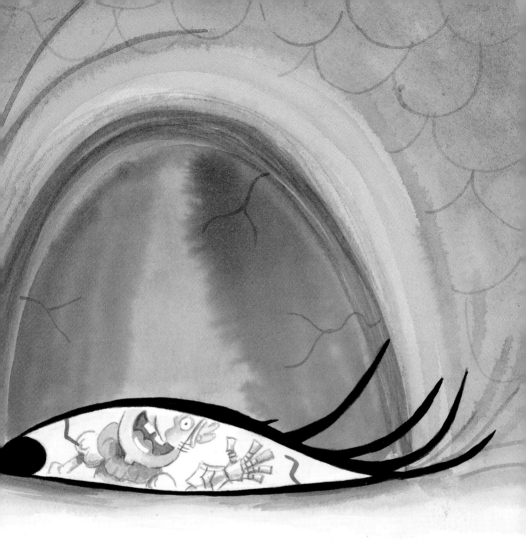

It went on ... and on ... and on.
The dragon closed his eyes.

When the dragon began
to snore, Sir Talkalot
had to stop.

The snore made his teeth rattle
so much that he couldn't talk!

The people in the village were delighted. The only problem was that now ...

29

... Sir Talkalot had yet another tale to tell!

Notes for parents and teachers

READING CORNER has been structured to provide maximum support for new readers. The stories may be used by adults for sharing with young children. Primarily, however, the stories are designed for newly independent readers, whether they are reading these books in bed at night, or in the reading corner at school or in the library.

Starting to read alone can be a daunting prospect. READING CORNER helps by providing visual support and repeating words and phrases, while making reading enjoyable. These books will develop confidence in the new reader, and encourage a love of reading that will last a lifetime!

If you are reading this book with a child, here are a few tips:

1. Make reading fun! Choose a time to read when you and the child are relaxed and have time to share the story.

2. Encourage children to reread the story, and to retell the story in their own words, using the illustrations to remind them what has happened.

3. Give praise! Remember that small mistakes need not always be corrected.

READING CORNER covers three grades of early reading ability, with three levels at each grade. Each level has a certain number of words per story, indicated by the number of bars on the spine of the book, to allow you to choose the right book for a young reader:

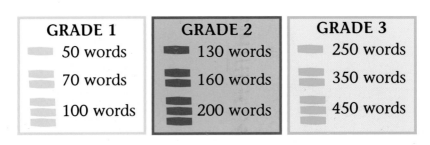

GRADE 1	GRADE 2	GRADE 3
50 words	130 words	250 words
70 words	160 words	350 words
100 words	200 words	450 words